Dear Parents:

Congratulations! Your child is taking the first steps on an exciting journey. The destination? Independent reading!

STEP INTO READING® will help your child get there. The program offers five steps to reading success. Each step includes fun stories and colorful art or photographs. In addition to original fiction and books with favorite characters, there are Step into Reading Non-Fiction Readers, Phonics Readers and Boxed Sets, Sticker Readers, and Comic Readers—a complete literacy program with something to interest every child.

Learning to Read, Step by Step!

Ready to Read Preschool–Kindergarten
• big type and easy words • rhyme and rhythm • picture clues
For children who know the alphabet and are eager to begin reading.

Reading with Help Preschool–Grade 1
• basic vocabulary • short sentences • simple stories
For children who recognize familiar words and sound out new words with help.

Reading on Your Own Grades 1–3
• engaging characters • easy-to-follow plots • popular topics
For children who are ready to read on their own.

Reading Paragraphs Grades 2–3
• challenging vocabulary • short paragraphs • exciting stories
For newly independent readers who read simple sentences with confidence.

Ready for Chapters Grades 2–4
• chapters • longer paragraphs • full-color art
For children who want to take the plunge into chapter books but still like colorful pictures.

STEP INTO READING® is designed to give every child a successful reading experience. The grade levels are only guides; children will progress through the steps at their own speed, developing confidence in their reading.

Remember, a lifetime love of reading starts with a single step!

Step into Reading, Random House, and the Random House colophon are registered trademarks of Penguin Random House LLC.

Visit us on the Web!
StepIntoReading.com
rhcbooks.com

Educators and librarians, for a variety of teaching tools, visit us at RHTeachersLibrarians.com

ISBN 978-0-7364-2860-6 (trade) — ISBN 978-0-7364-9029-0 (lib. bdg.)
ISBN 978-0-385-38350-9 (ebook)

Printed in the United States of America
10 9 8 7 6 5 4 3 2 1

Disney·PIXAR

MONSTERS, INC.

Boo on the Loose

By Gail Herman

Illustrated by Scott Tilley,
Floyd Norman, and Brooks Campbell

Random House 🏠 New York

Sulley worked
at Monsters, Inc.
His job was
scaring children.

Monsters went through
bedroom doors
to scare kids.

The whole city ran

on energy from screams!

Late one night,
Sulley saw a door
on the Scare Floor.

Sulley was confused.
He opened the door
and peeked inside.

It was a girl's bedroom.
The girl entered
the monster world!
Her name was Boo.

Sulley was afraid
of Boo.
Children were toxic
to monsters!

Sulley took Boo
to his friend Mike.
Mike was not happy.
Boo scared him, too.

Mike had a plan.
They would leave
Boo in the park.

They went to the park.

Boo stayed in the car.

She locked the doors.

Mike and Sulley
could not get in!

Then Boo saw
a butterfly.
She got out
of the car.

The butterfly flew
into the woods.
Boo chased it.

Mike and Sulley
had lost Boo!
Mike wanted to leave.

But Sulley did not want
to follow the plan.
Sulley liked Boo.

Mike went to the car.

It would not start!

Sulley had a new plan.

Boo's scream

would start the car!

Sulley ran
into the woods.
He would find Boo.

Boo was happy

to see Sulley.

Boo gave Sulley
a big hug.
They were friends.

Sulley and Boo
found Mike.
He was waiting
in the car.

Sulley smiled.
Boo did not
scare him now.

Sulley and Boo
got back in the car.
They still needed
Boo's scream.

But Boo was smiling.
Sulley did not want
to scare her.

Mike was mad.

He bumped his head

on the steering wheel.

The horn went *honk*!

Boo laughed.

Her laugh

started the car!

Mike was happy.

Sulley was happy.

Boo was happy.

It was time to go home.